F
GUARANTEED WAYS
TO ESCAPE DEATH

FORTY-NINE  WAYS to ESCAPE DEATH

poems by

SANDY MCINTOSH

MARSH HAWK PRESS
EAST ROCKAWAY, NEW YORK
2007

Copyright © 2007 by Sandy McIntosh

All rights reserved. No part of this book may be reproduced in any form or by any means, electronic or mechanical, including printing, photocopying, recording, or by any information storage or retrieval system, without permission in writing from the publisher.

FIRST EDITION

Marsh Hawk Press books are published by Poetry Mailing List, Inc., a not-for-profit corporation under United States Internal Revenue Code.

Cover and interior design: Claudia Carlson
The text of this book is Warnock Pro, the display is Trajan Pro.

Printed in the United States of America

LIBRARY OF CONGRESS CATALOGING-IN-PUBLICATION DATA

McIntosh, Sandy
  Forty-nine guaranteed ways to escape death / Sandy McIntosh. — 1st ed.
    p. cm.
  ISBN-13: 978-0-9792416-1-1 (pbk.)
  ISBN-10: 0-9792416-1-8 (pbk.)
  I. Title. II. Title: 49 guaranteed ways to escape death.
PS3613.C54F67 2007
813'.6—dc22
                          2007000783

MARSH HAWK PRESS
P.O. Box 206
East Rockaway, New York 11518-0206
www.marshhawkpress.org

Acknowledgments

Alimentum: "Escape From the Fat Farm"

Apple Valley Review: "The Shop Across the Street"

Barrow Street: "Ode to Jose in Japan" (as "Ode To Japan")

Galatearesurrects: "Eileen Tabios, Intestines. (Leipzig: Univ. of University Press. 2070)"

"Argol Karvarkian, Otiose Warts. (Bergen: Univ. of University Press. 2006)"

"Sandy's Mother Reviews *The After-Death History of My Mother* (East Rockaway: Marsh Hawk Press 2005)"

Hamilton Stone Review: "A Rare Visit To My Father's Office"

Logolalia: Ars Poetica "How The Work Gets Done"

Mobius, The Poetry Magazine: "A Ten Thousand Dollar Bill"

Otoliths: "Forty-Nine Guaranteed Ways To Escape Death"

Sentence: "Insignificant Meetings With Remarkable Men"

The New Verse News: "Their God"

Thanks, always, to Thomas Fink for his editing, and to Barbara for correcting Tom.

Contents

I. FROM THE CATALOG OF PROHIBITED MUSICAL INSTRUMENTS 1

Illustration from La Nature, *1883, depicting the cat piano described by Father Athanasius Kircher in his 1650* Musurgia Universalis. *In order to cheer up an Italian prince, a musician arranged cats in cages, so that when a key on the cat piano was depressed, a sharp spike drove into the appropriate cat's tail. The result was a melody of meows that became more vigorous as the cats became more desperate.*

1. The Octuba 3
2. The Novelty Concert Piano 4
3. The Tandem Flute 5
4. The Musical Scaffold 7
5. The Multiple-Percussive Timpani 9

II. INSIGNIFICANT MEETINGS WITH REMARKABLE MEN 11

Detail from "The Four Traitors," woodcut, 1845. Rhode Island Whigs who supported radical Thomas Wilson. Library of Congress.

Insignificant Meetings with Remarkable Men 13

III. EXCAVATED TRIREMES 21

Detail of an ancient trireme from Le Antichità di Ercolano (The Antiquities Discovered in Herculaneum), *published 1744–1792.*

I Channel Truman Capote 23
In a Dark Alley 25
The Old Men 27
The Shop Across the Street 30
Triremic Odes 32
A Snowball 34

IV. FORTY-NINE GUARANTEED WAYS TO ESCAPE DEATH   35

"Saved by Death," a convict escapes in a coffin. Wood engraving published in Police News, *May 19, 1877. State Library of Victoria.*

Forty-Nine Guaranteed Ways to Escape Death   37

V. AT THE FUNERAL HOME BAR   43

Combination of: "One Flag–One Country—Zwei Lager," federal soldiers in a tavern with their table replaced by a period coffin woodcut. Library of Congress.

A Ten Thousand Dollar Bill   45
Their God   47
On Contemplating Thomas Fink's *No Appointment Necessary*   49
College Memory   50
My Favorite TV Show of All Time   51
Good Wishes   52
How the Work Gets Done   53
At the Funeral Home Bar   55

VI. ESCAPE FROM THE FAT FARM   57

Detail from "Tweed-Le-Dee and Tilden-Dum," by Thomas Nast. Harper's Weekly, *July 1, 1876.*

Escape From the Fat Farm   59

VII. THREE URGENT REVIEWS 63

The Davenport brothers and William Fay with their spirit cabinet, circa 1908. Houdini wrote these mediumistic manifestations were "complicated exhibitions involving the use of a cabinet, rope tricks, bells, and various horns and musical instruments." Library of Congress.

1. Eileen Tabios, *Intestines*
   (Leipzig: Univ. of University Press, 2070) 65
2. Argol Karvarkian, *Otiose Warts*
   (Bergen: Univ. of University Press, 2006) 66
3. Sandy's Mother Reviews *The After-Death History of My Mother*, by Sandy McIntosh
   (East Rockaway: Marsh Hawk Press, 2005) 71

VIII. ESSENTIAL INVENTORIES 75

"The Men in Possession–Taking the Inventory." Crimean War cartoon, Punch, *October 13, 1855.*

Partial Inventory of List Poems Not Included in This Volume 77

Six Intriguing, Newly Discovered Verse Forms I've Decided To Share, After All 80

About the Author 83

I

From the Catalog of Prohibited Musical Instruments

From the Catalog
of Prohibited Musical Instruments

1. *The Octuba*

The conductor
of a symphony orchestra
built the *Octuba,*
after his own design.
A weird musical instrument
it requires eight strong men
and women to play it.
Its music
is *basso profundo in extremes,*
and its vibrations
dislodge bricks
in adjacent buildings.
People in the streets
fear earthquake.

It is rarely played,
and remains illegal
in twenty states
and the District of Columbia.

2. The Novelty Concert Piano

Edward Clement, Inventor: "Back in the '20s we made a special piano for orchestras touring the hinterlands. This piano had a lot of built in extras to amuse the hicks. It could chirp like a bird, croak like a frog, or boom like a thunderclap. It could laugh and shriek in a hilarious human voice, cluck like a chicken, howl like a dog in heat, or even produce water closet noises.

"By mistake we shipped one to Carnegie Hall.

"Paderooosky played it with the Symphony. Midway through the *Solemn Requiem,* he discovered the special controls and had great fun cranking them up all at once for a riotous climax.

"I understand the audience loved it, but Carnegie Hall complained, so my employer threw me out, along with my piano.

"They don't make pianos like that now, and I think you'll agree these techniques of piano manufacture are better forgotten."

3. The Tandem Flute

Two musicians,
who face each other

and blow
into each end,

play the silver
Tandem Flute.

The instrument,
only a half-meter

in length,
is capable of making

delightful music,
but the players

themselves
are often uncomfortable

staring into each other's
eyes

at short range.
This has led to violence.

In 1876,
the acknowledged masters

of the instrument,
Phil Wundt and Harvey Fechner,

settled a long standing
disagreement

when Wundt blew
a poisoned dart

through the barrel of the flute,
killing Fechner.

Following this,
as a matter of law,

hooded or blind
performers only may

play the instrument.

4. The Musical Scaffold

Before inventing
the electric chair
Thomas Edison

proposed
a moral cautionary
for mass executions:
the condemned
would be hanged
from ropes
braided of metal
instead of hemp.
Each would be tuned

to a different
note, and,
as bodies

dropped through
trapdoors
in sequence,
a solemn musical
composition
would sound.

If
hanging a party
of four,

the ropes would play
the portentous
opening notes

of Beethoven's
*Fifth
Symphony.*

If
a party of eleven,

the ropes could
be tuned
to play
*"Fear not
my friends,
for the worst
is yet to come."*

As an economical
alternative,
Edison proposed

that criminals
be hanged
from church bells,

their bodies, descending
and ascending
as the bells swung,
ringing

the musical
changes.

As Edison was mostly deaf, it is improbable
that he had any serious understanding of music,

anyway.

5. The Multiple-Percussive Timpani

As Pyotr
Illyich
Tchaikovsky featured
live cannon fire
in his *1812 Overture* Op. 49,
so the anonymous, hooded composer
of the *Fallujah Suite*
has given contemporary realism
to his composition
by including a deadly modification
of the orchestral Tympani.

In this composer's plan,
remotely controlled units
are hidden in secret locations
of the audience.
When activated these instruments
produce the sounds
and shock waves
of actual roadside bombs.

The composer has instructed
that the audience,
including those with heart conditions,
not be informed
about the presence of his *Multiple-Percussive Timpani*
so that the performance
may be climaxed
with authentic
"collateral damage."

—*for Ariana (a.k.a. Chloe)*

II

Insignificant Meetings with Remarkable Men

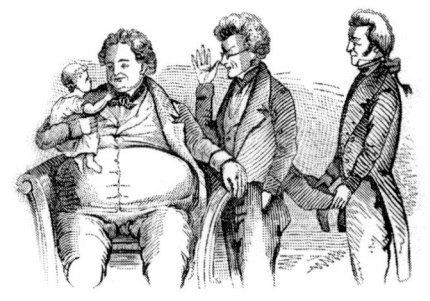

Insignificant Meetings with Remarkable Men

"The un-readiness is all."
—attr. G. I. Gurdjieff

1. My father knew General Eisenhower. I was three or four. He took me to meet the ex-president during half time at a Colgate vs. Army football game. "How are you, my boy?" Eisenhower asked, patting my head. "I have to wee-wee," I supposedly answered. He bent down and supposedly confided, "I do, too."

2. On Fifth Avenue, on the way to the "Merry Mailman" kiddies' television program, waiting to cross the street with my father, I pulled the gun out of a big cop's holster. The cop whipped around while my father stood back. "Gimme that, you little bastard!" I was upset that the cop had shouted, and so probably cried.

3. The Great Someone-Or-Other, (once-famous magician now performing at children's parties) tried to amaze us with a trick in which you drop shredded newspaper into a cake pan, light it, then cover it, say the magic words and a real cake appears!

I was smarter, though; I had my own
magic kit. I rushed to the stage
and unmasked
the cake pan's false
bottom. I received no applause,
and the magician looked
sad.

4. The principal of my Progressive school had a persistent fascination with Alain, a classmate from Haiti. "It's the chicken guts," Alain told me. "Everyone in my family tells the future by chicken guts." According to Alain, the principal would call him from his classes and they would meet under the apple tree, where the principal would question Alain about the divination of the stars and the planets. Alain asserted: "He believes everything I tell him." The principal was a stern disciplinarian and nobody's fool. But years later I heard he'd been fired, losing the school's money in inexplicable transactions. Reportedly, he pinned the blame on his personal oracle.

5. The summer before I was sent to military school my father introduced me to an older boy who attended there. Grown up, the boy is now a well-known real estate tycoon, owner of gambling casinos, and a famously angry star of his own TV show. At school, he was always nice to me, though he never laughed at my jokes.

6. Our military school chaplain was a war hero, credited with killing many men, though a priest. One afternoon, he caught me under the library smoking cigarettes. He ordered me to his office, reappearing in military uniform. I expected a tongue-lashing. Instead, he

marched me to the commandant's office, whining:
"This boy! A member of my religious instruction
class!" The commandant awarded me one hundred
punishment tours to be marched in dress uniform, a big
M-1 rifle on my shoulder. I never respected the chaplain
after that. He used to close his sermons with quaint
New England expressions, such as "Keep your peckers
up, boys." He'd seem bewildered when we'd laugh at
him, gleefully taking his good wishes the wrong way.

7. At fourteen,
my father dead,
I traveled to England
entranced by the novels of P.G. Wodehouse.
I thought I'd meet the famous writer there,
but someone told me
Wodehouse lived in America—
only an hour from my own town!
Home again, I looked up his address
and wrote to him.

He answered in one line:
"Sorry. I never met your father."

8. I attended college in the Hamptons, home of many
painters. The Abstract Expressionist, Willem de
Kooning taught elementary painting. "It's lonely in the
winters," de Kooning told me. "It was either teach with
your friends in the daytime or get drunk with them
at night, and end up in jail." Once, at his studio on an
errand, I'd brought my girlfriend. De Kooning offered
me a tall glass of Scotch. Then on the wagon, he insisted
on watching me drink. When I'd finished, he rubbed
his hands together. "Well, now," he said as he looked

at my girlfriend. "Well, well, well!" And he grabbed for her, chasing her around the studio. We fled soon after, despite his kind offer to show us his latest paintings.

9. With Chiara, the ten-year-old daughter of a friend living in Venice, I crossed the bridge to Ezra Pound's home. Chiara and Pound played chess now and then. Pound and Olga Rudge, met us at the door. Though supposedly in his silent period, Pound was full of conversation. "We play all the time. She always beats me," he told me. "But do you play?" I didn't. Silent then, he turned and headed for the chess table. Olga Rudge made me a cup of Lapsang Souchong tea. "He loves his game," she told me. Crossing the bridge on the way home, I asked Chiara how it had gone. "Beat him, as usual."

10. A year later I returned to Venice. The last boat for Il Cemetario was leaving and I'd just had time to catch it. Pound had died, and was buried near the graves of other idols: Igor Stravinsky and Serge Diaghilev. I'd only begun to search for them when, behind me, a bell pealed. I turned and saw the great wooden doors of the cemetery closing. I escaped but had seen nothing I'd come to see.

11. As a student at Columbia, I was given plum assignments, escorting visiting writers around the campus. I met Jorge Luis Borges, the blind aristocrat poet, at his subway stop, and offered my help. His translator and aide, Norman Thomas di Giovanni answered for him: "Thanks, but we can find our own way. After all, I went to school here." Later, I was asked to help the famous poet and communist, Pablo Neruda, to the airport. "No need," his driver told me. "He'll take his limousine."

12. "One knew other poets when one was at university," W. H. Auden told us on a visit to our classroom. "But one would never expect to find them in such an odd thing as a Creative Writing class." Auden was wearing a blue terry cloth bathrobe and sipping a Martini. (I can't be sure of this.) He proceeded to denigrate all poetry except traditional meter as a means for teaching students. He offered to help us learn the classical forms. I don't know how many students returned for his next class. Being a modernist, I didn't go.

13. At the Cathedral of St. John the Divine, they were dedicating the Poet's Corner. Later, Robert Penn Warren stopped me in the street. He'd been a guest of honor at the ceremony, but now wanted directions to the subway. I did my best to be detailed and exact. After all, he was an old man and might get lost. I even offered to ride with him to his destination. When I'd finished my detailed instructions he replied: "No, I think I'll take a cab."

14. Jean Erdman, wife of Joseph Campbell, had produced a play by a friend of mine. At the reception held at their apartment, I ran into Campbell on the balcony, gazing at the twilight sky. What a wonderful chance; however, I'd read none of his books. "Nice evening," he observed with his familiar lisp. I agreed that it was, indeed, a nice evening. He turned and walked back inside.

15. Years after I'd been his student, I became a teaching colleague of the only poet on the English department faculty. We had been good friends, but he'd betrayed me. "How many poets do you think *can* be on an English department faculty?" he asked after he'd blocked my tenure. I was angry, plotting revenge. Not till years

later did I see a chance for it. My enemy had become deformed with Parkinson's, his arms festooned with bandages. "It's the drugs," he complained. "When I dream, I act out. Last night I punched my fist through the window." Now, in my triumph, I felt nothing but pity—no pleasure at all.

16. I published a long poem about a writer I'd known in graduate school, a terrific manipulator. Thoroughly self-centered but brilliant, he often disparaged my projects, claiming that I shouldn't be surprised as I was "the competition." At a book fair, years later, where my new book was on display, I was staggered when he appeared in person, walking down the aisle. He had aged, but over the years had gained national fame and respect from readers and other writers. I was sitting behind the counter, watching him approach. Without noticing me, he examined my book in familiar head-tilted, birdlike posture. I was thrilled that he might buy my book! I imagined his surprise when he'd begin the poem and instantly recognize himself! He stared for a time at the book cover, but walked away without saying anything.

17. Trying on a leather jacket,
    I told the clerk: "A few silver studs
    would make it look really cool."

    "The stud,"
    he replied,
    "is *inside* the jacket."

    I admired myself in the mirror
    wearing the leather jacket:
    taller, leaner, sexier—dangerous!

What a revelation!
The real me: a remarkable man!
I saw my new life:
wild successes,
overmastering men,
seducing women.

However, the jacket turned out to be too expensive,
so I bought a different one.

>   *—for Denise Duhamel*

III

Excavated Triremes

I Channel Truman Capote

The Petulance of the Deceased:

Well, let me see...
Do you have any peanut butter?
I think I might like to spread some
on a cracker.
My, you seem to have
a large collection of bric-a-brac.
Nick-a-nac.
Is there a theme here?
Or is it all random stuff
you found in the street?
I like this one especially:
the plastic palm tree
with the sign
"Welcome to Brooklyn."

What kind of host are you?
Standing all-agog.
If you're expecting me to say something witty
then you've picked the wrong moment.
It's certainly dusty in here.
I think I'd like a glass of something.

*

The Omniscience of the Deceased:

The winning number is 3741823.

Put your money on Lubricious Sister in the 8th race at Santa Anita.

Just use some lemon juice.
The stain will come right out.

No. She doesn't love you anymore. Doesn't even think of you.

How tedious you are.

*

The Moral Righteousness of the Deceased:

Yes. I did visit the house in Sagaponack on New Year's Eve. There were boys I knew living there. I was disappointed when you answered the door. I was in a funk and sat down on the couch and didn't stir for hours while you and the boys reveled at some poor poet's party. And during that time I absolutely did not do the nasty things you claim in that defamatory—if happily unpublished—essay.

But, meanwhile, you got ripping drunk and spun your car on the ice, nearly killing everyone. Nauseating, your behavior, really. I recommend you throw away that essay, in which you pretend to be the hero, and print this one, instead.

In a Dark Alley

three male perps molesting
someone I couldn't quite see.
I was hesitant,
silent in shadows.

Then, at the brightly lit street
entrance, Superman appeared.
His arms thinner, his physique less
formidable, yet he hoisted each molester
over his head
and threw him headfirst
onto the ground,

a cigarette
depending
from his lips.

*

I should have told him:
"Thank you, Superman." or "Thank you, Man of Steel."
(I'd forgotten the correct form of address).

*

But, anyway, he shrugged, avoiding eye contact,
as if to clarify that,
in the end, our talents are modest;
we only do what we can do.
And here was a man who,
at the first sign of trouble,
could throw on a cape
and smash miscreants into concrete.

He must have been relieved
that I didn't make a big deal of it.
He seemed anxious to get out of there,
back to feeding the cat or sipping a cappuccino
before his singular talent again
called him into the shadows.

The Old Men

Awkward With Hays

H.R. Hays,
was never anything
but kind to
me. Yet,

I was uneasy
with him. Over the
years, when I'd bring my
poems,

we'd
exchange desultory
words, but then lapse
into painful

silence.

I never
knew whether to address
him
as "Professor" or
"Mr. Hays"

or "Hoffman" when he'd
answer my calls.

So, I'd just
say my name without

saying his. I
don't know

if this made him
uneasy,
thinking me so self-
involved I couldn't
even acknowledge
him.

It certainly made *me* uneasy.

Years after his
death his daughter
surprised me
when she said, "I don't know

if you knew it,
but my father considered you
his closest friend."

   —for Penny

*

Ignatow Wearing My Shirt

It is the end of June, Friday, the weekend before a holiday. I remember years ago, on a blazing day like this, living on Springs Fireplace Road surrounded by painters, poets. Growing up with literalists, as I had, those without attention for anything but advancement in school, business, a rubber-stamped family, etc.—what a gift it was!

Today, I re-read your final book, in it, your

conversation with your imminent ending, and find
myself no longer a kid, but a middle-aged man
who's ending must also be considered. I listen to
your voice, pristine despite the elapsed years.

In the author's photograph you're smiling. You're
wearing my brown plaid shirt that I'd left at your
house when I stayed overnight. I liked that shirt.
I wish I had it to wear again. But in any case, it
achieves our conversation.

—*for David Axelrod*

*

A Rare Visit To My Father's Office

I don't think I'd ever seen him in action, giving a
presentation to colleagues. Later, I sat close by. He really
was a handsome man, but with a dueling scar that I
didn't remember.

"What I wanted was to be articulate,
to be on a stage addressing millions,"
he lamented. "But you see
how I've tied my fingers in knots?
Unlike your generation, we rarely had a public forum."

True. We, living, hog the spotlight, our authorized
biographies in every stupid song, our faces on every
milk carton, our full names in answer to any question
you care to ask.

Still it was nice to see Dad, one grownup to another.
Now he was articulate about his shyness, his
ambivalence about having once been alive.

The Shop Across the Street

First it was a shoe shop.
    The shoemaker so poor,
he slept on the floor
    and resoled customer's shoes
with cardboard.

*

When it was a clothing store
    the young owner
decorated her window
    with grace and invention,
one spring hanging a sign
    "Just Married!"
and posing manikins
    as bride and groom
holding pictures
    of her own wedding.
Another spring
    her sign read:
"It's a boy!" and she dressed
    her manikins
in blue
    surrounding them
with toys.
    For Halloween,
she costumed the manikins
    with sinister masks.
But in December,
    when she dressed them
in Christmas finery,
    she neglected to remove
the sinister masks—

       which troubled us
as we ate our breakfast
       and watched
from the café across the street.
       Later, she hung a sign:
"Divorced. Closing Store."
       She'd stripped the window
and abandoned the manikins
       to their nakedness.
Under the stark
       neon streetlamp
they glared at us:
       Arctic snow.

*

Now the shop
       is run by a man
selling buttons.
       He has swiveling reptilian eyes
and dresses formally,
       a lengthy metal chain
from a window curtain
       as a watch fob
on his polka-dotted vest.

       —for Peter Blair

Triremic Odes

Ode to José in Japan

We're standing at the base of Mt. Fuji, the landscape dense with fog and clouds. "Where is the mountain?" asks our friend, José.

José is a refugee from Cuba. He's never seen the world. Now, improbably, he's here with us in Japan.

"Sometimes there is a mountain," intones Mike Heller, reminding us of the old Zen *koan*. "And sometimes there isn't a mountain."

But I suspect there's something mercenary going on. "Mt. Fuji is not here today," I suggest to José. "The Japanese tourist board moves it to different parts of the country where there are tourists willing to pay to see it."

José considers, then observes: "This part of America, I think it is really strange."

*

Ode to My Aunt's Hands

She had been a concert pianist
for sixty years.

The skin of her hands
was translucent.

I thought I could see
the bones and sinews within

as if they were submerged twigs and grasses
at the bottom of a pond.

No matter how fast or slowly
her fingers moved over the keys,

the pond rippled gently,
uninterrupted

by the musical notes,
that, like fishes,

were swimming within.

*

Ode to Incense

Two sandalwood incense sticks
laid out in their long burner:

legs of a soldier in a red coat
on her deathbed.

As she reaches extinction
she clutches her ashen boots.

Smoke gathers,
a final great billowing.

She lifts herself into it
by her bootstraps.

A Snowball

Ginsberg threw a snowball
at Frank O'Hara's coffin
at the bottom of the grave.

"Damn," he whispered.
"Damn, damn."

*

"A lovely, sentimental story," Ginsberg told me.
"But not true. Frank died in July. Not much snow.
Who told you this?"

"Armand Schwerner, I think."

"Well, Schwerner wasn't there."

*

In time,
I imagine Ginsberg's grave.

Nothing sentimental about it:
It's a warm day, early April,

the grave is opened,

a snowball
balanced

on its edge.

IV

Forty-Nine Guaranteed Ways to Escape Death

Forty-Nine Guaranteed Ways to Escape Death

1. Aunt Elizabeth didn't believe in death. "Just go up to the coffin and sprinkle water on his face. He'll wake right up. You'll see; they always do."

2. Wes, my cab-driving colleague told me that the first thing his mother invariably said upon viewing the deceased was, "My, doesn't she look healthy?"

3. Eileen Tabios' father died on April 11th, my father on April 10th, my brother on April 9th, and Burt Kimmelman's mother on April 3rd. Our calendars are filling up. Under the new rules, only one person you know is allowed to die per day. After the 365th there will be no more death.

4. Ron owned the funeral home where most of my family had been laid out. I'd begun to consider him my personal mortician. One day I met him at the bank. "I sold the business," he told me. "My friend and I were born the same day. We turned sixty. My friend dropped dead at our birthday dinner. It shocked me. I'd never really thought about death, I guess." He had to do something, he said, so he was going skiing.

5. Joseph Heller's character, Yossarian cultivated boredom to prolong his life. The actor, George Saunders' suicide note read: "I was bored."

6. In the end, Carlos Castaneda, unable to burn with "the fire from within" implored his disciples to "intend me

forward. Intend me forward!" beyond death. But despite his disciples intentions, he died. He was cremated. Later, his disciples told the world that he had not died at all. Instead, he had entered the realm of the "third attention." They continue to defend their belief against all. "Intend!" they shout at their doubters. "Intend! Intend!"

7. A lesson from *Scientific American*, 1980: "We used to believe in the particle theory [of light], but now we believe in the wave theory, because all who believed in the particle theory have died."

8. On Halloween night, 1982, at Sleepy Hollow cemetery in Upstate New York, two boys found a newly opened grave, tunneled to the adjacent one, opened the coffin and propped the corpse of a woman against the tombstone. The next day, as the funeral of the husband began, relatives were amazed to discover his dead wife posed as if awaiting his arrival. "She always said she'd see the old man dead," a relative recalled. "I just didn't know how she'd pull it off."

9. From an Internet story: "Yes, I realized, my patented Acme Hero Anti-Death Suit had saved my life yet again."

10. Bessie the Cow, our childhood pet, her brass bell clanging merrily as she moos: Moo, moo. No dear, we don't eat the cow. We eat the beef, the boeuf, the steak, the fatted calf. No, not the calf. We eat the veal. And not the bah, bah lamb but the mutton. And not the bunny but the lapin, the hare, the game. We hunt, and it's not only for the eating but also for the immortality to be found in transubstantiation of fish into seafood, pig into pork, and deer into venison. But when there's no game afoot, when there's famine in the land, then

there remains only Bessie the Cow. How do we separate Bessie from the children, and the children from the starkness of the moment? We take the merry bell from Bessie's neck, lead her to the barn, and send the children home. "Cheeseburgers for dinner!" we promise.

11. Fred told his friend he napped eight times a day and enjoyed a long night's sleep, as well. "Why waste your life that way?" asked his friend. "There'll be plenty of time to sleep when you're dead." "Ah," answered Fred. "But when I'm dead there will no longer be time to dream."

12. When my friends and I were young we watched horror flicks on midnight TV. *Dracula, Frankenstein, The Wolfman* and *The Mummy*. From these we learned that to cheat death one must become a stalking, devouring monster. On the third day, when the rock was rolled from Jesus' grave, his friends must have been terrified.

13. When George complained to a religious friend that, no matter how much he had prayed, his father had not come back from the dead, as Jesus had promised. "You have only to wait for the right time. It could be one year, or one thousand years. Just wait." George's heart was uplifted. "Thanks," he told his friend. "I didn't know you could do that. I'll just sit right here until it happens."

14. Houdini visited the graves of family members and magicians constantly, examined the long-dead bodies of his father and brother when they were exhumed, and once traveled out of his way to see the burned bodies from a schoolhouse fire. As someone remarked: "For a man who had resurrected himself so many times, how strong a barrier could death be?"

15. Don't bury your old loves. They'll drag you into the ground with them. If you can't let them drift up into the sky, at least run with them through the forest of your longing.

16. "The earth is suffocating," wrote Frederic Chopin at the end, in 1849. He begged his friends to have his chest cut open so that he wouldn't be buried alive.

17. A method to avoid live burial, 1850: A pull cord is built into the coffin. It runs to the top of the grave and thence to a bell. Should the occupant awake after burial he need only pull continuously on the cord to ring the bell, which will serve as an alarm. The caretaker, should there be one present, will hear the bell and then re-open the grave, releasing its occupant."

18. When all seems lost, write a letter to your departed loved one and pay to have it printed on the obituary page. Apparently, the deceased read obituary pages, judging by how many letters to them are printed. Now the problem is to figure out which newspapers your own departed ones read.

19. "They sell charms here that ward off death," said Katya, my Grecian beauty. She told me they are blue with an eye painted on to deflect death. You wear them on a necklace or a bracelet. According to Katya, the poet Homer is said to have worn one on his forehead and warned his enemies: "I may be blind but I've got my eye on you!" She said you could also purchase a blue bead to wear instead of an eye. Blue is the color that wards off the death-stare, but it is also commonly thought that blue-eyed people are exceptional givers of it. "So beware when a blue-eyed person pays you a compliment, it could be your last," she warned. *(However, modern*

science has proved that death can result from the actions of people of other eye colors, as well. —ed.)

20. Grandfather cautioned: "Don't grow old!" I promised I wouldn't.

21. [*Highly questionable immortality scheme redacted.*]

22. We took a high school art trip to the Guggenheim Museum. They were showing the French Impressionists. At the top of the long spiral gallery was a painting by Van Gogh, "Starry Night." A man glared at me. He leaned over and hissed, "I'm standing right here so you better not make fun of my painting!" I didn't realize until later that if he really was Van Gogh he must have been well over 150 years old. Also, he'd grown his ear back.

23. Two Recipes: For Death, construct an effigy of yourself. Go to the cemetery and get some dirt. Try to do this during a waning moon, when the moon is in Scorpio or Capricorn. Construct a small box. Light a black candle. Put the effigy into the box. Bury it in the graveyard. Do not think about the spell as this will interfere with its working. For Life, reverse these instructions.

24. Do not open this door. Do not open that door. Do not open the door over here, or the door over there. Or the inside door. Or the outside door. Neither the porch door, nor the front door. Neither the closet door, nor the refrigerator door. You don't need to know what's behind Door Number One, or Door Number Two, or Door Number Three. Don't open the door marked "Private." Don't open the door marked "Come In." Don't open the trap door. Don't open the fire door. Don't open the coffin door.

25. Do not live at home. Most fatalities occur in the home.

26. Make your last day at least 25 hours long.

27. Be too goddamn mean to die.

28. My children (if I had any) tug at my shirtsleeve. "Daddy," they beg. "Please don't die." Although I do not have children, I promise them anyway: "I won't die. I'll stay alive. For you."

29. Make a list like this, but don't stop.

V

At the Funeral Home Bar

A Ten Thousand Dollar Bill

A woman asked if I could change
a ten thousand dollar bill.
I told her, "Nobody can change
a ten thousand dollar bill."
But I opened my wallet anyway
and found that I had ten
one thousand dollar bills.
"It's your lucky day!" I told her.
"Here's your change."
She gave me a wink
and a big smile.

Later that day
another woman asked me for change
of a ten thousand dollar bill.
I told her, "Nobody can change
a ten thousand dollar bill."
"But I just saw you change one this morning," she argued.
"Won't you open your wallet again and look?"
So, I opened my wallet,
and, yes, there was change
for a ten thousand dollar bill.
"It's your lucky day!" I told her.
"Here's your change."
However, counting it out
I noticed that the first ten thousand dollar bill
wasn't in my wallet. I'd never taken it
from the first woman!

I ran back to the first woman,
who was still smiling and winking.
"I've spent it all," she said

in answer to my question.
And now tears filled her eyes.
I felt sorry for her
and opened my wallet
to give her the second
ten thousand dollar bill.
But my wallet was empty!
I quickly realized
I'd never put the second
ten thousand bill in my wallet!

I ran back to where the second woman stood.
"I've spent it all," she told me
tears filling her eyes.
I patted her hand.
All I could do was stand there
holding her hand.

Eventually, I found
comfort for myself:
Even if I'd had
the ten thousand dollar bill,
it wouldn't have done me any good,

because nobody can change
a ten thousand dollar bill.

Their God

One afternoon, their God announced that he would destroy the world. (Someone had made a silly joke about him and, as usual, he'd taken umbrage.) "I could wipe you off the planet with my snotty hankie, or burn you with my cigar," he thundered. "Instead, to teach you a lesson, I'll do it in a way you'll understand." He announced that he would build an explosive device of incomprehensible destructive power. Then he roiled the sky with red and blue theatrical lights, swirling clouds. From out of the sea he arose to confront us, his splendid figure magnificently muscled, standing almost seven feet tall, and wearing a peek-a-boo loincloth.

Then he disappeared into our city. We heard that he'd set up shop in an old barn. Someone saw him at the dump, scavenging parts from discarded televisions. He even came to our door to borrow a screwdriver. A month later, the rumor was that he'd taken a job pumping gas in order to pay the rent on a larger workshop. We trembled at the thought of his huge bomb nearing completion and of the horrendous consequences to follow. We'd already packed our bags, withdrawn our savings from the bank, and let the cat out.

Months passed without cataclysm. The newspaper reported that he had made a speech at a Rotary Club dinner, and the mayor had suggested that he might do well in politics, perhaps becoming a judge. The big factory he'd built at the edge of town for his bomb construction was the second largest employer in the county. He was becoming a community big shot, always smiling and throwing kisses when you'd meet him in the street. It was rumored that the leading political party wanted to draft him for the mayor's job. Anyone could see that he was enjoying himself. Gradually, we began to relax, tentatively unpacking our bags.

But still the threat of imminent annihilation was there like an annoying insect, buzzing and biting when you'd least expected it. We didn't know whether to renew our magazine subscriptions or pay the cable bill. "Why torture us this way?" I asked my wife when the newspaper hinted that he might be secretly dating a movie star. "Why doesn't he just get it over with?" My wife mused, "There's something about these immortal beings," she said. "They're thinking, 'Screw 'em! We've got all the goddamn time in the world.'"

On Contemplating Thomas Fink's
No Appointment Necessary

Lately, I find I'm only interested in people
who remind me of people
I was once interested in. And new music
only holds me
when it reprises old music.
And I am bored by overheard conversations
of teenage girls, office workers,
laborers, etc. which simply restate
everything—which is eating and screwing.
It's hardening of the categories. Age,
awareness is suffocating, but Tom says:
"Virgin scissors may / claim
anybody's oxygen lantern."
Then says: "Ceilings are
wonderful parents
blessed with / oil."
That's it, Tom says;
the way out—that-a-way, he says:
Like Ezra Pound Hercules
straddle the centaur:
Make it nude.

College Memory

Some party! Toilet smashed,
sink dismembered.

I awoke beneath the potted cactus.
It took fifty pairs of pliers

to extract the needles!
Then my roommate shouted:

"Things are happening with a vengeance!
It's nothing but *Crime and Punishment* out there!"

I hid in the basement with my cheat sheets
waiting for the final exam—
a cigarette between my teeth, like Roskolnikov,
smoking myself into murderous frenzy.

—for Michael Zwerling

My Favorite TV Show Of All Time

A beautiful collie watches me from the other side of the TV screen.

You could look into her eyes and imagine all sorts of adventures:

>the time she saved the boy from the abandoned well;
>the time she saved the boy from the abandoned mineshaft.

You could look deeper and find something wordless, ancient:

the Ur dog. What company sponsored that show?

All I know is that my friends and I gnawed on dog bones for years.

Now, Mother tells me she has to go out.

"Don't leave the room," she warns.

"If you do, that big dog will get angry."

I look at the dog: she's seemingly asleep.

Gathering my courage, I stand up.

But the dog is instantly up, too, growling, barking, clawing the screen, and showing fearsome teeth.

Terrified, I sit down. After a moment, the dog sits.
Soon she is yawning, her eyes closing.

But it is enough: I know now that she will always be watching me, even in reruns.

Good Wishes

I felt her hands on my face.

It was the middle of the night.
"You're burning up," she said.
"Would you like a cold towel
for your sunburn?"

"Thanks," I told her.
"But don't get up. I'll be okay."

"It's no trouble," she answered.
"I've just got one for myself. See?"

I looked over
but saw no towel anywhere.

"I'll get one for you, too,"
she sighed. "They're so refreshing."
Then she rolled over
and began to snore.

  —for Barbara

How the Work Gets Done

I challenge my dream: "Show me the Equator. I've never seen the Equator." And I'm there, registering at a hotel on some tropical island in the middle of the ocean. I look around expecting the exotic but everything looks depressingly ordinary, as if this were some grubby convenience store in Canarsie. "Show me things I've never seen," I command my dream. I'm imagining succulent equatorial flowers, blossoms billowing like parachutes, and juicy fuchsia-hued fruits big as boulders.

The scene changes, but instead of embroidered nature, I find myself in the hotel's unremarkable cocktail lounge. Some guests have dressed formally. Others are naked. We're just a bunch of people sipping our drinks, probably waiting for dinner. We attempt conversation, but it goes nowhere. "This is nothing," I scold my dream. "Show me the horrors, the spectacular horrors of the Equator!" I'm imagining spiders towering like skyscrapers on stick legs, and malevolent vampire insects numerous and unremitting.

Nothing outwardly changes, although, one by one, I begin to recognize my fellow guests. In fact, I realize that I know every one of them and I wouldn't voluntarily spend a second in their company! I notice, too, that everyone now is looking around the room and recognizing everyone else. From their gloom I surmise that everybody has discovered universal, mutual hatred.

Can it be that, compelled by the rules of civility, we must spend our short, once-in-a-lifetime equatorial vacations in this Sartrean hellhole in intimate contact with those who revolt us?

But then it dawns on me: "Thank you," I tell my dream. "For this true horror of the Equator!"

At the Funeral Home Bar

This funeral home is impressive, shiny new, vast as a convention hall, coffins and mourners everywhere crowding the horizon. Over there, the dancing Hassidim; yonder, the phlegmatic Peloponnesians. Every religion, every class is accommodated. But I'm here on business. I roll my mother's wheelchair toward a couple of idle morticians. "Could you watch her for a moment?" I ask. "I've got to meet someone at the bar." "Certainly," they answer. I can tell they're about to give me that creepy mortician smile that says: *You don't know what we know about what happens next.* However, I don't have time to humor them. I've got business at the funeral home bar—

— which turns out to be a lovely place, warmly lit and crowded with genuine, friendly folk. No rude barroom jocularity here. Indeed, they make quiet, respectful jokes. Occasionally one will place a comforting hand on another's shoulder.

I've come here to meet my friend, but time passes and she never shows up. "Your friend is late? Get it? She's your *late* friend?" says the gentleman next to me. I laugh politely. "Don't worry," he says. "Sooner or later she'll show up. They always do."

But she doesn't, so I decide to head home. Once off the barstool and onto the floor, I realize that everyone here is extremely tall. Even I seem to be taller than when I came in. "Mourning will do that to you," says the gentleman next to me. "Sadness does it. Let me show you," and he makes a sweeping gesture with his hand. The scene is transformed. We're no longer affable people at a funeral home bar but tall pine trees in a forest. It is winter. The air is clear, cold. And though we stand together, each of us is somber and alone.

VI

Escape from the Fat Farm

Escape From the Fat Farm

DAY 1: "Cappy", our dining room host, announces: "You'll be served delightful low-calorie meals, and you *shall* lose weight!"

DAY 2: I gaze at my plate. The solitary pea that was on the edge has rolled over the rim and disappeared.

DAY 3: Cappy says beware the alligators in the moat. And keep hands off the rabbits. Delectable, yet their bites are deadly.

DAY 4: The table talk has turned entirely to food—if at breakfast, then about lunch. If at lunch, then about dinner. Then breakfast again. We are insatiable in our talk about food!

DAY 5: We suspect Little Tubby Moran has caught and eaten a rabbit. Our jealousy knows no bounds.

DAY 6: We've been debating the best method for capturing an alligator. "Can you whistle and they come?" No. "Can you call them: 'Hey, alligator! Hey, alligator!'?" No. "And would pan roasting be easier, or stuff it whole into the oven?" Probably neither. "I'd rather have the shoes, belts and handbags," observes adorable Penelope, but the rest of us know the truth. She'd wrestle an alligator to death, its fritters steaming in the sun, if they'd just let us out of this building.

DAY 7: Our conversations are now whispered because Cappy is watching and listening, his hands clanking metal ball bearings, like Captain Queeg. He is definitely suspicious of our whispering.

DAY 8: The meals get no better. A slight diversion: our waiter, a new daddy, shows off his infant child. This event leaves us quiet, meditative. Our tablemate, Dr. X, an admitted amateur torturer, opines that cleaning, cooking and eating a human infant is as simple as cooking a baby pig. We find this horrible and disgusting, and we tell him so. But this leads to speculation on where we might find a baby pig.

DAY 9: Cappy now appears each night dressed as a pirate, complete with wooden leg. He twirls his pirate's gun and reminds us by certain gestures that it's loaded.

DAY 10: Someone serves us the wrong dinner! The menu said Steak with Mashed Potatoes and a Chocolate Milkshake! But all we got was a plate of spoons! Not even a steak knife! Little Tubby Moran complains loudly, but answer gets he none.

DAY 11: We are served a bowl of murky soup made with moat water. An openly hostile Cappy commands: "Get in there with your spoons and row, you blackguards!" And he fires a warning shot across our bow. It is understood that we must now address him as "Captain."

DAY 12: Little Tubby Moran has disappeared. Nobody says it, but we're all thinking the same thing: *cannibalism*. Dr. X is missing, also.

DAY 13: There is open talk of mutiny. The captain has chained us to the deck. We're fed only low-fat yogurt with the occasional strawberry floating in it. But all we need is the opportunity and Cappy goes down. Then we'll row ourselves across the moat to freedom and a good brunch.

DAY 14: A terrible storm at sea. Cartons of croutons and little packets of mayonnaise float by, but always out of reach. Penelope says: "Let's see if we can swim as far as the kitchen. I'll get a decent meal if I have to kill someone!" We manage this, and are awed. Refrigerators, their shelves weighed down with food, loom. And there is something else. In the blackness a lone figure stands between us and our dinner. It is Cappy aiming his pistol. "I'll take care of this," Penelope hisses, darkly determined. "This night we eat!"

DAY 15: Morning sun and quiet sea. At last, it's all over. Cappy has vanished. The dining room doors have opened. We, tattered survivors, pull ourselves together. Outdoors, a bucolic scene: alligators dozing like armored cars on the moat banks; sounds of tiny sprockets turning inside the bodies of caterpillars. And as we're led to the scales, we discover to our delight that we have lost weight, exactly as advertised in their brochure, though it's mostly arms and legs.

VII

Three Urgent Reviews

1. Eileen Tabios, *Intestines*
(Leipzig: Univ. of University Press, 2070)

Eileen Tabios' newest manuscript, *Intestines*, is impacted with ellipses that join what appear to be incoherent concepts, such as *foreskins* with *fishhooks*, and *flatulence* with *phlebitis*. That is, they are incoherent at first. But reading on, one surmises a relentless inevitability in this work's construction. Those little dots between the words are not voids at all, but tiny, albeit multidimensional furnaces wherein the meaningless pairings are forged into inseparability. Tabios' process is isomorphic with the modern physical theory of wormholes in space, through which a traveler may find an instantaneous shortcut to a destination of unimaginable distance. This is alarming. Science is only beginning to explore these things with appropriate delicacy and forbearance. Tabios, not a scientist, is creating a terribly dangerous threat by persisting in this direction. I have always been against censorship, but in this case, at the edge of the deadly unknown—the unknowable—I urge that this literary work not be published. In my considered opinion, it should not even be written.

2. Argol Karvarkian, *Otiose Warts*
(Bergen: Univ. of University Press, 2006)

This forty-fifth collection continues Karvarkian's obsession with miniature poetics: lyrics gorgeously wrought, each with the grace and identicalness of a Fabergé egg. It is curious that after Karvarkian's decades of writing and publishing well-mannered volumes, his many readers may not recall his earliest work, which is characterized by a surprisingly primitive, even brutish sensibility. A far cry from the lapidary encrustations of his contemporary work, his earlier poems seem to have originated in a swamp: metaphors dense as quagmire, often expressed in grunts, such as "Bleep. Fsssssh. Poof." Contrast this with the minimalist clarity and grace of a lyrical refrain from a poem in his newest collection: "This. That. This."

I first met Karvarkian in Florida. I had recently married, and my wife and I shared a shack on stilts in an obscure part of the Everglades, where I could work on my literary criticism in solitude. Karvarkian was young, of course, with massive, unkempt hair and musky odor. The three of us became friends after we'd met at the local fishing-themed bar in town. Gradually, I began to notice the attraction Karvarkian and my wife shared, and so I wasn't surprised when one day he took me aside and growled, "I'm leaving on a lengthy journey to reach the end of the world. And, oh yes, do you mind if I take your wife?" He was surprised, I surmise, by my gracious accession.

There then seemed to be an endless supply of wives in the Everglades, so I had no trouble marrying again. What did astound me, however, was that within a month of my second marriage Karvarkian reappeared, his long trip apparently cut short. He pointed his finger at my trembling first wife. "I don't like this one," he told me. "But your new one seems entirely lovable. Do you mind if I take her along on my infinite journey?" Naturally, I protested greatly! Wasn't one enough for him? But my new wife flashed her eyes and they hurriedly departed.

This left me in rather an awkward position. My first wife and I were no longer properly married, but she didn't seem to be leaving the house, so we resumed our cohabitation with the proviso that I might at any time, should I wish to, take a new wife. Eventually I did.

It was then that Karvarkian once again reentered our lives. "Take this one back," he ordered, thrusting my second wife at me. "Lemme have the new one." Numbed, I could only allow her to go.

Now I was living with two former wives. After some time, I remarried. Moments after that ceremony, as if he'd been lurking beneath a trap door, Karvarkian abruptly appeared demanding the new wife in trade for the old.

This pattern continued for some years. Eventually I stopped protesting because I'd begun to notice that after each exchange of wives a new book of Karvarkian's poetry would appear. Each time, I would read it with immense interest and greatly marvel at his progression of intellect and technique from volume to volume.

His eighteenth collection, *Phlogiston You Bet,* evidences what we might call the typical Karvarkian poem of the early middle period: distinctive language and budding obsession with the mysterious shadow figure, eventually to be known as the Procurer, so famously developed in later volumes:

*A can of f*****g beer*
*collides with a f*****g cold thought:*
Pimp me vittles,
*that little b******d*
better deliver
*me f*****g flame-retardant*
flapdoodle another beer
*in f*****g skirts*
*or I crush his f*****g*
smooch. ("A Bone Aren't Made of Beer")

By his thirtieth volume, *We'll Burn That Bridge Before We Invent It,* his outlandish verbosity has given way to a diction both natural and unforced:

The notion of amber gosling
waddling, My sainted Procurer
in his red wheelbarrow.
"Ducky," I coo. "Get me another
in her flowing skirts. This one's gone dry."
Gosling nestles, but tiresome Procurer
demands recompense.
Grudgingly,
I flip him the bird. ("The Pushover Prize")

Although I support forty-six ex-wives on the meager receipts of my modest critical efforts, I can't help but believe that I had something to do with the great Karvarkian's evolution as a poet. After all, he seemed to extract a tangible grace from the women I married—and, I flatter myself—possibly because of my own connection to them. I'd also like to think that my judiciously crafted critical prose, which my wives have assured me they read aloud to him each evening, helped to discipline his earlier poetic unruliness.

I can think of no better evidence of this than this latest volume. Here he demonstrates, with a directness characteristic of his formative earlier work, what may be a final, summative reconciling with the Procurer, the mysterious shadow-figure:

Needles, needles.
Glockenspiel headstrong.
Ale may ail and skirt hurt,
but o my sissy-brother,
there is nary the consumer
absent the consumed. ("Elapsed Bumbershoot")

Whether this mysterious Procurer will ever be brought fully from the shadows must wait on future Karvarkian collections, although much good criticism has already appeared. (See my *The Mysterious Procurer in the Poetry of Karvarkian*. Three volumes. Freemont: Univ. of University Press. 2004)

Still, if we are to consider the totality of Argol Karvarkian's oeuvre, we must ask, what does it signify? What will be its influence? These beautiful Faberge egg-like poems, a dozen to a package: how are we to understand such exigent fragility? I think, in the end, they will share the fate of all delicately created things. Like Faberge eggs they will abide as objects that we can admire, but that, once having admired, we relegate to the collector's shelf without further thought.

3. Sandy's Mother Reviews *The After-Death History of My Mother*, by Sandy McIntosh
(East Rockaway: Marsh Hawk Press, 2005)

He was always a disappointment. He should have run a bank, but he barely passed math. He should have been a wealthy lawyer, but he leaves his fly open and stutters in public. Look how he misinterprets my good intentions when I find these nudie pictures in his room:

*

My mother had rummaged through my room, never saying a word, leaving the naked pictures there for me to know she knew I had them. I was never beyond her grasp. Private parts would never be private. She herself was a greater force of nature than even adulthood, and we both knew her name was Silence. ("Private")

Well, boo-hoo. I like things to be in order. How did I know how ungrateful he'd be each time he came home and discovered I'd rearranged and repainted his room? These were acts of love! Then he goes about copying down my senile remarks as if they were just the cutest things! For instance:

The hospital parking lot is empty.
My mother's in her favorite chair refusing to speak.
"Such a character," laughs her roommate.
"She touches you and tells you you are healed
and may go home."
Her roommate hands me a pamphlet

> *with favorite quotations of my mother*
> *assembled by the other patients:*
> *a collection of libelous rumors concerning my wife and me.*
> *One passage, supposedly from Jesus, reads:*
>> No one knows what will happen
>> when I leave my tomb in the night
>> to touch you. ("The Hospital Chair")

He's nothing but a plagiarist, a poseur.

In another poem he has me sleeping in the snow after I supposedly wander away from an Alzheimer's institution. I was never in an Alzheimer's institution. And I've never slept in the snow! Then he says he dumps me in the Public Library where they videotape me each week until:

> ... *I was told that the library's funds had run out*
> *and my mother's project would be terminated.*
> *I would never see my mother again,*
> *since over time she had become an image on a screen,*
> *and the library would pull the plug.*
> ("The After-Death History of My Mother")

Well, in his favor, he does get something right:

*We lower my brother's coffin
beneath his monument.
Abruptly, mother hisses: "Look!"
Not twenty feet away,
another monument,
the grave of my brother's nanny.
"She wanted him for her own," mother whispers.
"Now she's got him."*

*A decade passes.
The game of Cemetery Chess progresses slowly.
Mother dies; her monument
erected midway between brother and nanny.
As we lower my mother down
I whisper to the nanny: "Check."*
("Cemetery Chess")

It's justice that we keep the old bitch at bay. Still, I resent him using me, prying open my coffin, looking around inside, touching things, moving them. It's a cheap way of making a buck. Even this book review I'm supposedly writing strains credulity.

Remember that film *Psycho*? Well, that's him, my son. He's put on his mother's dress and he stabs at me with that horrible knife!

VIII

Essential Inventories

Partial Inventory of List Poems Not Included In This Volume

1. Animals I Have Eaten

2. Eighty-Eight Failures of the Imagination

3. One or Two Things Everyone's Completely Forgotten

4. A Deconstruction of "One Hundred Bottles of Beer on the Wall"

5. A Typology of Hallucinations

6. Primeval Insomnias of Foam (Ivan V. Lalic)

7. Passwords that Rust in the Mouth Like Useless Keyholes (Ivan V. Lalic)

8. Body Parts Sorted by Spiritual Merit

9. Machines that Reduce Objects to Their Actual Size

10. Four Hundred Fifty-Nine Guaranteed Ways To Escape Death

11. Fossil Forms of Thought

12. The Twelve Secrets of Successful Polygamists

13. Adorable Nicknames for the Constellations

14. James Tate's Curses Upon "All Those Who Do or Do Not Take Dope"

15. Wittgenstein's Methods for "Bridging the Abyss Between Individual Numbers and the General Proposition"

16. Fifty Good Reasons Why Your Deceased Relatives Have Better Things to Do Than Pass Judgment Every Time You Screw Up

17. The Complete Inventory of List Poems Not Included in this Volume

18. Several Reasons Why You Don't Want to Give Your Little Boy or Girl a Doll Called "Bugger Me, Elmo"

19. Forty-One Words that Will Dislocate Your Jaw if Spoken Too Loudly or Too Rapidly

20. Holy People I Like Because They Share My Point of View

21. This List in Etruscan

22. Eighteen Things Supposedly Too Subtle to Mention

23. Thirty-Three Famous Writers and Artists Whom I May Have Met But Don't Have Any Interesting Stories About

24. Six Intriguing, Newly-Discovered Verse Forms I Won't Be Sharing With Other Poets

25. Nineteen Extremely Uncomfortable Sexual Positions

26. The Complete Catalog of Prohibited Musical Instruments

27. Embalming Recipes For the Home Chef

28. The Very Simple Chores I Neglected to Do Before the House Collapsed

Six Intriguing, Newly Discovered Verse Forms I've Decided To Share, After All

1. *The Petite Mirabeau-d'age*—Inspired by the Eighteenth Century French writer and statesman Honoré Gabriel Riqueti, comte de Mirabeau. Worried that he had failed to establish his name in literary perpetuity, Mirabeau retreated to composing in a sophisticated variant of the French language of his own invention. Few could understand it, but those who could greatly admired the flexibility of its alphabet, which was composed of just six letters. Hence, the *Petite Mirabeau-d'age* refers to an *abecedarian* (alphabet-guided) verse form utilized by those challenged by alphabets containing a larger number of letters.

2. *The Lesser Padeuteria*—A poem giving thanks to our Adjunct English Department faculty for what we have been taught, or to God for our Adjunct English Department faculty. Like its cousin, the *Padeuteria*, it is a genre that, according to Richard A. Lanham in his *A Handlist of Rhetorical Terms*, "has often suffered from neglect but cannot be too strongly recommended."

3. *The Lion's Moan*—Both a *lament* and an *abnegation* composed in one line or less. It originated with Buddhist monks who, failing to attain Enlightenment after a lifetime of practicing mistranslated sutras, sought revenge by robbing banks in America's Old West.

4. *The Trireme*— An ancient and obscure poetic form, named after the Greek fighting ship designed to cover long distances quickly under three sets of oars. Its rules

of composition are too complex to go into here, save to point out that it has an affinity with the ancient Malay seafaring form, the *Pontoon*.

> (**Editor's note**: We hasten to alert the reader to the dubious historical validity of the author's claims above. In the *Trireme* examples he provides elsewhere in this volume, we find no consistent *schema* of composition, except that the author has divided them into three parts to suit his own conveniences. We also strongly suspect that his claim of that form's affinity with a Malay nautical verse form called the *Pontoon* is only the author's mendacious misquotation of *Pantoum* or *Pantun*, a Malay verse form with many historical examples, few having anything at all to do with the sea.)

5. *The Retrograde Novena*—A poem of two sets, each with nine lines, composed one line per day for eighteen days, the first nine preceding a great holiday, and the second nine following. Echoing its musical counterpart, the *Retrograde Inversion*, in which an imitative voice sounds notes both backwards and upside down, the first nine entries preceding the holiday record moments of great joy one expects to share with one's family, while the second erases each of the preceding lines, substituting the moments of vexation that one has actually experienced.

6. *The Christmas Calendar Poem*—Similar in intention to the *Retrograde Novena*, the *Christmas Calendar Poem* is a poem of twenty-four lines written on the face of a traditional *Christmas Advent Calendar*, and expresses good wishes for all one's friends and acquaintances. However,

hidden beneath each good hope
is a paper trapdoor
under which is inscribed
specific tortures
one feels should be inflicted on these people.

On Christmas day, the author,
in a private ceremony
celebrating the primal instincts of poetry-making,
opens the trapdoors.

About the Author

SANDY MCINTOSH's collections of poetry include *The After-Death History of My Mother, Between Earth and Sky* (Marsh Hawk Press), *Endless Staircase* (Street Press), *Earth Works* (Long Island University), *Which Way to the Egress?* (Garfield Publishers), and two chapbooks: *Obsessional* (Tamafyhr Mountain Poetry) and *Monsters of the Antipodes* (Survivors Manual Books). His prose includes *Firing Back*, with Jodie-Beth Galos (John Wiley & Sons), *From A Chinese Kitchen* (American Cooking Guild), and *The Poets In the Poets-In-The-Schools* (Minnesota Center for Social Research, University of Minnesota. His poetry and essays have been published in *The New York Times, Newsday, The Nation*, the *Wall Street Journal, American Book Review*, and elsewhere. His original poetry in a film script won the Silver Medal in the Film Festival of the Americas. He has been Managing Editor of *Confrontation* magazine published by Long Island University, and is Managing Editor of Marsh Hawk Press.

Other Books from Marsh Hawk Press

Norman Finklestein, *Passing Over*
Eileen Tabios, *The Light Sang As It Left Your Eyes*
Claudia Carlson, *The Elephant House*
Steve Fellner, *Blind Date with Cavafy*
Basil King, *77 Beasts: Basil King's Bestiary*
Rochelle Ratner, *Balancing Acts*
Corinne Robins, *Today's Menu*
Mary Mackey, *Breaking the Fever*
Sigman Byrd, *Under the Wanderer's Star*
Edward Foster, *What He Ought To Know*
Sharon Olinka, *The Good City*
Harriet Zinnes, *Whither Nonstopping*
Sandy McIntosh, *The After-Death History of My Mother*
Eileen R. Tabios, *I Take Thee, English, for My Beloved*
Burt Kimmelman, *Somehow*
Stephen Paul Miller, *Skinny Eighth Avenue*
Jacquelyn Pope, *Watermark*
Jane Augustine, *Night Lights*
Thomas Fink, *After Taxes*
Martha King, *Imperfect Fit*
Susan Terris, *Natural Defenses*
Daniel Morris, *Bryce Passage*
Corinne Robins, *One Thousand Years*
Chard deNiord, *Sharp Golden Thorn*
Rochelle Ratner, *House and Home*
Basil King, *Mirage*
Sharon Dolin, *Serious Pink*
Madeline Tiger, *Birds of Sorrow and Joy*
Patricia Carlin, *Original Green*
Stephen Paul Miller, *The Bee Flies in May*
Edward Foster, *Mahrem: Things Men Should Do for Men*
Eileen R. Tabios, *Reproductions of the Empty Flagpole*
Harriet Zinnes, *Drawing on the Wall*
Thomas Fink, *Gossip: A Book of Poems*
Jane Augustine, *Arbor Vitae*
Sandy McIntosh, *Between Earth and Sky*
Burt Kimmelman and Fred Caruso, *The Pond at Cape May Point*

Marsh Hawk Press is a juried collective committed to publishing poetry, especially to poetry with an affinity to the visual arts.

Artistic Advisory Board: Toi Derricotte, Denise Duhamel, Marilyn Hacker, Allan Kornblum, Maria Mazzioti Gillan, Alicia Ostriker, David Shapiro, Nathaniel Tarn, Anne Waldman, and John Yau.

For more information, please go to: **http://www.marshhawkpress.org**.